Are We Still Friends?

by Ruth Horowitz

illustrated by Blanca Gómez

Scholastic Press New York

Beatrice and Abel

lived side by side,

with a low stone wall between them.

Abel grew apples.

Beatrice raised bees.

They were the finest of friends, indeed.

And so were the bees and the trees.

In summer, when honey filled Beatrice's hives, she hollered, "Halloo, Abel! You free?" and he crossed the low wall to help gather the sticky, sweet liquid.

In autumn, when apples filled Abel's trees, he called, "Halloo, Bea? Please?" and she crossed the low wall to help harvest the ripe, red fruit.

In winter, the bees and the trees rested.
So Beatrice and Abel rested, too.
Side by side, they spread crispy toast with
apple butter and sipped warm tea with honey.

Beatrice and Abel needed each other all year,
but especially in springtime, when Abel's trees
filled with flowers.

Beatrice's bees needed flower nectar to make their
honey. Abel's trees needed bees to spread their pollen
to make their fruit.

Back and forth across the wall the bees flew,

until . . .

One spring morning — *WHACK!* —
Abel smacked into a branch. "OUCH!"
The smack startled a bee. *ZING!*
The bee stung Abel right on his nose.
"YOWWW!" Abel yammered. "WHEE
HEE HEE!"

Across the wall, Beatrice heard
Abel squeal.

What a silly laugh, she thought.
"Wheeee! Heeee! Heeee!"
she laughed back.

Was Bea laughing at him?
Abel wondered.
He rubbed his sore nose.
"Blasted bee!" he bellowed.

Was Abel talking to her? Beatrice wondered.

"Don't you bellow at me," she yelled. "Pie Face!"

"Pie Face?" Abel sputtered. "Well, you're a . . . Fuzz Brain!"

"Wormy Core!"

". . . Fuzz Brain!"

Back and forth the words flew, until
Beatrice and Abel marched into their houses
and slammed their doors behind them.

There sat Abel, his hurt ripening like a big, round apple.

"Pie Face?" he spluttered. "I don't need her or her bees!"

And there sat Beatrice, her anger buzzing like an irate insect.

"Fuzz Brain?" she muttered. "I don't need him or his trees!"

But outside, the bees continued their quiet business.
Back and forth across the wall they flew, sipping
nectar and spreading pollen, just the same as always.

Abel scribbled a sign and planted it where
the bees would see it.
But the bees didn't care about that sign.

NO BEES
ALLOWED

Beatrice built a fence to keep the bees
on her side.
But the bees didn't care about that fence.

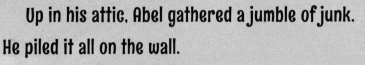

Up in his attic, Abel gathered a jumble of junk.
He piled it all on the wall.

Down in her basement, Beatrice found a mishmash
of trash. She stacked it on Abel's jumble.

NO BEES ALLOWED

"Sour Apple!" Beatrice snarled.

"Fuzz Brain," Abel answered.

And you know what the bees did.

But Beatrice and Abel didn't care.

Higher and higher, they stacked and piled,

until . . .

PLINK!

Something slipped.

CLINK!

Something dipped.

And with a clatter and a crash, the whole teetering mass tumbled into the bee yard.

What a mess!

In all that tangle, there wasn't a sign of Beatrice.

"Halloo?" Abel called.
No answer.
"Halloo?" Abel shouted.
Where was she?

Then he heard something. It could have been the bees or the wind in the trees. But it seemed to be coming from the pile. And it seemed to be saying, "Hallooooooo . . ."

"Halloo?" Abel called. "HALLOO?"

At last, Abel found her.

"Halloo, Bea!" he whooped. "I thought I'd lost you."

"Halloo, yourself," she croaked. "I thought you didn't care."
Abel offered a hand and helped her climb out.

"I thought you were laughing at me," he said. "I'm sorry."

"I thought you were insulting me," she said. "I'm sorry, too."

"Are we still friends?"

"Indeed!"

They looked at the yard. What a royal mess!

"I'll put everything in apple pie order," Abel promised.

"I'll help," Beatrice said.

So, side by side, they cleaned everything up.

Back in Abel's kitchen, they spread crispy toast
with apple butter and sipped warm tea with honey.
"We're numbskulls," said Beatrice.
"Mush minds," Abel agreed.
They were the finest of friends, indeed.
And so were the bees and the trees.

ho

ney

Beatrice

Abel

Just the same as always.

Easy Apple Butter Recipe

2 pounds apples (about 7 or 8 apples, depending on size)
1 cup apple cider
3/4 cup sugar
2 teaspoons ground cinnamon
1/8 teaspoon allspice
1 tablespoon lemon juice
1 tablespoon vanilla

WITH THE HELP OF A GROWN-UP . . .

Peel, core, and chop apples.

Add apples and cider to heavy saucepan and bring to a boil.

Reduce heat and simmer for 20 minutes.

Add remaining ingredients and stir to combine.

Return to boil, reduce heat, and simmer for 30 minutes or
        until apples are tender. Cool slightly.

Mash apples with a potato masher or put in a food
        processor to blend.

Let cool. Spread on toast and enjoy!

Store in an airtight container in refrigerator.

For Theo. — R.H.   To my friend Pablo, who lives side by side with me. — B.G.